Willy Whitefeather's River Book for Kids

ROBERTS RINEHART PUBLISHERS
BOULDER, COLORADO

ROBERTS RINEHART PUBLISHERS
6309 Monarch Park Place
Niwot, Colorado 80503

Manufactured in the United States of America

10 9 8 7 6 5 4 3 2

Library of Congress Cataloging-in-Publication Data

Whitefeather, Willy, 1935—
[River Book for kids]
Willy Whitefeather's river book for kids.
    p.   cm.
Summary: Choona, a young Cherokee boy, goes down the river in a canoe with his grandfather and learns many useful things which he will use throughout his life.
ISBN 0-943173-94-9
1. Cherokee Indians—Juvenile fiction. [1. Cherokee Indians—Fiction.
2. Indians of North America—Fiction. 3. Canoes and canoeing—Fiction.
4. Grandfathers—Fiction.] I. Title. II. Title: River Book for kids.
PZ&.W58496Wi 1994
[E]—dc20   93-38686

NOTE TO PARENTS SEE PAGE 123

THANKS! CHUCK LAUREL SARAH STAR

SPECIAL THANKS TO JEFF LOCKRIDGE 1ST WORLD'S GREATEST EDITOR

PART OF THE PROCEEDS OF THIS BOOK WILL GO TO HELP DISADVANTAGED NATIVE AMERICAN KIDS.

Willy WHITEFEATHER

WHAT'S IN THIS BOOK? SEE PAGE 121

THIS BOOK IS ABOUT
TWO RIVERS – THE RIVER OF **WATER**
AND THE RIVER OF **LIFE.**

I WROTE IT FOR **MY GRANDKIDS**
AND **ALL YOU KIDS,** TO HELP YOU FEEL
GOOD ABOUT **YOURSELVES** – SO YOU
LEARN **HOW TO GUIDE** YOURSELVES
AROUND **THE BOULDERS** ON THE
RIVER OF LIFE AND **KEEP ON**
PADDLING.

SO GRAB A PADDLE
AND LET'S GO – **EE-YAH!**

LONG AGO IN A **VILLAGE** BY A **RIVER** THERE LIVED  A **YOUNG CHEROKEE** BOY NAMED **CHOONA HUNTEH** (OR "FLOATS DOWN RIVER"). CHOONA LOVED TO **SWIM** AND **PLAY** AND **FISH** IN THE RIVER. AND ONE DAY CHOONA ASKED HIS **GRANDFATHER** IF HE COULD GO DOWN THE RIVER WITH HIM IN HIS CANOE.

"YES," SAID GRANDFATHER, "BUT YOU MUST **LISTEN** AND **DO AS I SAY— AGREED**?"
"**AGREED**," REPLIED CHOONA.
"VERY WELL, THEN I WILL **TAKE YOU**," SAID GRANDFATHER.

GRANDFATHER GOT IN THE **BACK** AND **STEERED**, AND CHOONA **PADDLED** FROM THE **FRONT**.
CHOONA'S YOUNGER BROTHER, **YONA**, WAVED AT THEM FROM THE **SHORE**.

2

GRANDFATHER SHOWED CHOONA
HOW **EASY** IT WAS TO STEER A CANOE
FROM THE **BACK** AND HOW **HARD**
IT WAS TO STEER FROM THE FRONT.
"WATCH THE RIVER CLOSELY,"
SAID GRANDFATHER. SEE HOW THE
WATER ROLLS UP AND BOILS ? THAT'S
AN **UNDERWATER BOULDER** THAT CAN

...CATCH AND **HOLD** A CANOE OR
TURN IT OVER OR **RIP OUT** THE
BOTTOM. WATCH FOR **RIPPLES**
THAT MEAN **SHALLOW WATER**—AND
LISTEN FOR THE **SOUND** OF THE
RIVER THAT COULD MEAN ...

3

...A **WATERFALL** UP AHEAD!

"A **WATERFALL** SOUND TELLS US TO **PADDLE IN** AND CARRY OUR CANOE AROUND **PAST** IT.

4

"PADDLE **HARD** AND **STRONG!**"
SAID GRANDFATHER WHEN THEY PUT
THE CANOE BACK INTO THE RIVER.

CHOONA COULD NOT SEE HIS
GRANDFATHER UNLESS HE TURNED TO
LOOK BACK, BUT GRANDFATHER'S
WORDS KEPT HIM **LOOKING AHEAD**
AND **WATCHING**.

AS THEY PADDLED ON...

CHOONA SAW THE **ROCKS** AND **TREES**
AND **EARTH** AND **SKY** AND **SUNSHINE**
SPARKLING ON THE WATER, AND HE FELT
THE **CALM** OF THE RIVER FLOW
THRU HIM.

"BACKPADDLE!"
SAID GRANDFATHER.

TWO **BIG** BOULDERS IN THE RIVER WERE COMING UP **FAST.** AS THE CURRENT CARRIED THE CANOE **TOWARD THEM,** GRANDFATHER STEERED THE CANOE SMOOTHLY **THRU** THE **TONGUE** OF **WATER** BETWEEN THE BOULDERS. "EEEEEEEEEEEEEEEEEEEeeee," SANG CHOONA SOFTLY, AS THEIR CANOE GLIDED PAST THE BOULDER ...

... AND INTO A CALM. GRANDFATHER STOOD UP IN THE CANOE SO THAT HE COULD SEE **FARTHER AHEAD** FOR ANY MORE **RAPIDS** OR **WHITEWATER.**

CHOONA THEN STOOD UP ALSO—BUT HE **LOST** HIS BALANCE AND **FELL** IN THE RIVER!

"HA-HA-HA," LAUGHED GRANDFATHER.

"HA-HA-HA," LAUGHED CHOONA, AS HE CLIMBED **BACK** INTO THE CANOE.

"BALANCE IS IMPORTANT," SAID
GRANDFATHER WHILE
CHOONA SQUEEZED
WATER FROM HIS HAIR.
"WE CAN **RELAX** NOW,"
HE TOLD CHOONA AS THEY CAME TO A
LONG, CALM STRETCH OF RIVER.
GRANDFATHER SHOWED CHOONA
HOW TO **QUIET PADDLE** THE CANOE
WITHOUT LIFTING THE PADDLE
OUT OF THE WATER

AND WITHOUT MAKING A SPLASH OR
SOUND, SO THEY COULD QUIETLY
COME UP ON . . .

... A **HERD** OF **DEER** THAT WERE DRINKING, SO AS **NOT TO SCARE** THEM AWAY.

CHOONA COULD ALMOST **REACH OUT** AND **TOUCH** THEM, BUT HE SAT **VERY STILL** AND DID NOT EVEN MOVE.

"VERY GOOD," WHISPERED GRANDFATHER, "YOU HAVE DONE WELL,"

AS THE CANOE GLIDED PAST THE DEER.

"THANK YOU, GRANDFATHER, FOR TEACHING ME SO WELL."

"CHOONA, I HAVE SHOWN YOU AS **MY GRANDFATHER** SHOWED ME AND AS **HIS GRANDFATHER** SHOWED HIM — FOR MANY TIMES YOUR FATHER MAY BE **TOO BUSY** HUNTING OR PLANTING CROPS TO SHOW YOU THE WAY OF THE CANOE AND THE **RIVER**.

"AS THE RIVER FLOWS ALONG SINGING ITS SONG ON ITS JOURNEY TO THE SEA, IT WILL **TELL YOU** ITS **SECRETS** IF ONLY YOU WILL **LISTEN!**"

SPRING TURNED INTO SUMMER AND CHOONAH HUNTEH **BECAME A MAN** AND ONE DAY HE WENT TO HIS GRANDFATHER'S CABIN.

AND HIS GRANDFATHER SAID TO HIM, "YOU HAVE **LEARNED WELL**, CHOONA. HERE IS A **GIFT** I HAVE CARVED FOR YOU."

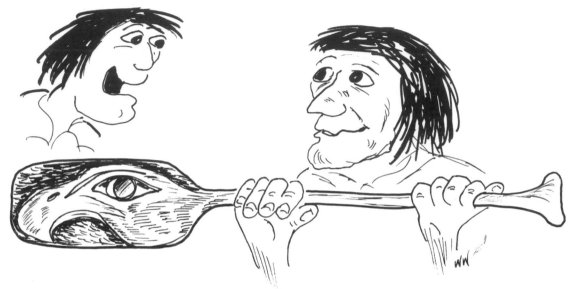

"A **WATERBIRD PADDLE!**" EXCLAIMED CHOONA, "IT'S TRULY **BEAUTIFUL**. THANK YOU, GRANDFATHER."

"AND BECAUSE YOU WILL NEED SOMETHING TO GO WITH THIS PADDLE,

HERE IS *MY CANOE*."

"*WAH-DOH* (THANK YOU), GRANDFATHER, YOU HAVE GIVEN ME *MUCH*."

"ONE DAY YOU WILL SHOW OTHERS HOW TO CANOE THE RIVER, AND WHEN THEY HAVE LEARNED WELL FROM YOU, CHOONA, YOU MUST TELL *THEM* TO SHOW OTHERS.

"IN THIS WAY KNOWLEDGE WILL *FLOW LIKE THE RIVER FLOWS—FOREVER* ...

"ALWAYS *RESPECT THE RIVER*. IT WILL MAKE YOUR SPIRIT **STRONG** AND WILL GIVE YOU **JOY**. BUT IF YOU SHOULD *EVER GO* **FOOLISHLY** AND **NO LONGER** RESPECT THE RIVER, IT CAN **DROWN** YOU!

"**TALK** TO THE RIVER AND IT WILL **TALK TO YOU**,

NOT IN **WORDS** BUT BY **SHOWING** YOU ITS WAYS, FOR AS EACH DAY IN **LIFE** IS NOT **THE SAME**, WHAT YOU LEARN FROM THE **RIVER** WILL HELP YOU ON THE **RIVER OF LIFE**."

"THANK YOU, GRANDFATHER, FOR THESE WORDS."

AS THE YEARS GO BY, CHOONA HUNTEH BUILDS HIMSELF A CABIN ABOVE THE RIVER.

ONE SUMMER MORNING
CHOONA'S BROTHER, YONA, WHO
LIVES IN THE CITY, BRINGS HIS
TWO KIDS, TINA AND DOOLEY,
OUT TO CHOONA'S CABIN.

"OH-SEE-OH (HELLO), CHOONA!"
YELLS YONA.
   "HI, UNCLE CHOONA!"
SHOUT TINA AND DOOLEY.
   "OH-SEE-OH AND HI BACKATCHA!"
HOLLERS CHOONA. "HEY, I'M REALLY
GLAD TO SEE YOU GUYS—C'MON
IN AND I'LL PUT ON A POT OF

BLACKBERRY TEA AND SOME
CORN BREAD.

"I HAVEN'T SEEN YOU
IN A **LONG TIME**, YONA, AND YOU
KIDS HAVE **GROWN A LOT**."
"THESE TWO HAVE BEEN
BADGERING ME TO BRING THEM
HERE TO SEE YOU. THEY WANT TO
GO **DOWN** THE **RIVER** WITH YOU,
CHOONA.

"I'VE BEEN LIVING IN THE
BIG CITY FOR SO LONG, I HAVE
FORGOTTEN MUCH OF THE
WAYS OF **THE RIVER**...

". . . BUT **YOU**, MY BROTHER, **NEVER LEFT** OUR GRANDFATHER'S LAND. YOU **KNOW** THIS RIVER **WELL** —AND NOW THAT THE KIDS ARE **OLD ENOUGH**, I FEEL THEY ARE **READY TO LEARN.**"

"OH YES! WE WOULD **LOVE TO CANOE THE RIVER** WITH YOU, UNCLE CHOONA!" CHIME IN TINA AND DOOLEY.

"WELL THEN, WE **WILL GO,** AND IT WILL BE A **GOOD RIVER TRIP,**"REPLIES CHOONA.

YONA'S EYES **LIGHT UP.** "THANK YOU, BROTHER.

I MUST **GO BACK** NOW TO MY **JOB IN THE CITY.**"

"GOOD YONA. YOU CAN MEET US IN 4 DAYS AT THE PLACE CALLED **RIVER RATS' ROOST,** AND YOU CAN HELP **HAUL THE CANOE** AND **SUPPLIES BACK** UP HERE," SAYS CHOONA.

"**NO PROBLEMA,** "REPLIES YONA, "SEE YOU ALL ON THURSDAY."

"**SEE YOU, DAD!** " YELL TINA AND DOOLEY.

AS YONA DRIVES AWAY,

THE SUN SETS BEHIND CHOONA'S CABIN.

CHOONA TURNS TO TINA AND
DOOLEY AND SAYS, "I KNOW YOU
KIDS ARE ANXIOUS TO GO, BUT
WE ALL NEED A GOOD NIGHT'S
SLEEP. LET'S **HIT THE SACK**

WHOMP!

SO WE CAN BE
ON THE RIVER **BY DAYBREAK."**
CHOONA, TINA, AND DOOLEY ARE
UP AT THE **CRACK of DAWN** ...

...AND THEY LOAD THE CANOE WITH **BEDROLLS IN A DRYBAG** AND **FISHING HANDLINES** AND A **FRY PAN** CHOONA STUFFS IT ALL UNDER THE SEATS.

THEN CHOONA SHOWS TINA AND DOOLEY SOME **LIFE VESTS** HANGING ON PEGS IN THE CABIN. "CHOOSE THE VEST YOU WANT TO **GO DOWN THE RIVER WITH...**"

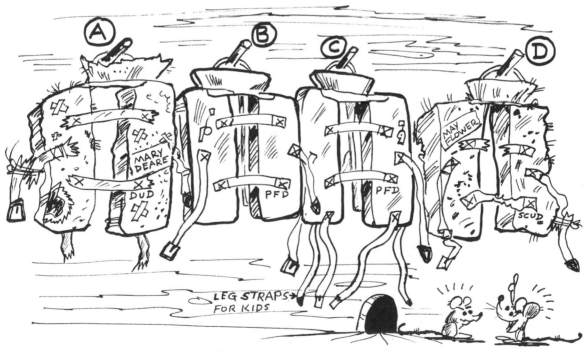

WHICH DID **YOU** CHOOSE?

"GOOD," SAYS CHOONA, "YOU BOTH MADE THE RIGHT CHOICE. YOU PICKED THE BEST VESTS, NOT THE OLD, WORN-OUT ONES. YOUR VESTS SHOULD FIT SNUG, BUT NOT TOO TIGHT, SO YOU CAN BREATHE AND PADDLE EASILY. "ALWAYS GO DOWN THE RIVER WITH THE BEST VEST, FIT JUST RIGHT FOR YOU, AND YOU CAN'T GO WRONG."

YOU TAKE THAT OFF THIS MINUTE!

"WHY DO WE **NEED LIFE VESTS**, UNCLE CHOONA?" ASK TINA AND DOOLEY. "WE **KNOW** HOW TO **SWIM!**"

"THAT'S GOOD," REPLIES CHOONA, "BUT IN CASE YOU GET **THROWN OUT** OF THE CANOE INTO RAPIDS, THE LIFE VESTS WILL **HOLD YOU UP** NO MATTER HOW STRONG THE CURRENT IS.

"JUST BE SURE TO **LAY BACK** AND **KEEP YOUR FEET IN FRONT OF YOU,** POINTING **DOWNRIVER.** THAT WAY YOUR **FEET** HIT ANY ROCKS YOU MEET, **INSTEAD** OF YOUR **HEAD.**"

WHICH WOULD **YOU** CHOOSE, Ⓐ OR Ⓑ?

IF YOU CHOSE Ⓐ, YOU'LL BE
ALL RIGHT!
"OKAY, KIDS. LET'S MAKE FRIENDS
WITH THE WATER.

"LAST ONE IN **CLEANS THE FISH**
WE CATCH!" YELLS CHOONA, AS HE
JUMPS INTO THE RIVER.

KER-PLOOSH! KER-PLASH!

TINA AND DŌŌLEY HIT THE WATER
AT THE SAME TIME, SPRAYING
CHŌŌNA. "**HEY-YAH!**" HOLLERS CHOONA.

"RIVER CURRENTS **LIKE TO SWEEP YOU AWAY** , SO BE SURE AND **STAY IN THE EDDY**, KIDS."

"EDDY?" ASKS TINA

"YES, THAT'S THE **CALM WATER NEXT TO THE CURRENT...**

" THE RIVER IS CALLED A **LONG PERSON.** IT'S ALWAYS BEST TO **MAKE FRIENDS** WITH THE **WATER** BEFORE WE START OUR TRIP. LET'S **GET TO KNOW** HIM."

THE RIVER IS CALLED A LONG PERSON

CHOONA **HOLDS** THE CANOE **STEADY** SO TINA AND DOOLEY CAN CLIMB IN.

"**GRAB YOUR PADDLES**. PUT ONE HAND **CLOSE TO THE BLADE** AND THE OTHER HAND **ON TOP OF THE HANDLE**.

HANDLE

BLADE

"**GOOD!**" SAYS CHOONA. "NOW, **TINA**, YOU PADDLE ON YOUR **RIGHT**, AND **DOOLEY**, YOU PADDLE ON YOUR **LEFT** LIKE ME. THAT WAY OUR PADDLES **WON'T BUMP** INTO EACH OTHER — AND WHEN WE GET TIRED, WE CAN ALL **SWITCH SIDES**."

DOOLEY

TINA

CHOONA

TINA'S HAND SLIPS DOWN THE HANDLE
JUST AS HER PADDLE HITS AN
UNDERWATER ROCK, AND...

THE HANDLE **BONKS** DOOLEY ON THE
HEAD.

DOOLEY'S IN PAIN, "**OOPS**," SAYS TINA.
"LET'S TRY THAT AGAIN," SAYS CHOONA.
"NOT WITH **MY** HEAD!" GROANS DOOLEY.
"I'M SORRY," SAYS TINA. "THAT'S OKAY," SAYS DOOLEY.

"LOOK," SAYS CHOONA, "MY HAND ON **TOP** OF THE HANDLE GIVES ME MORE POWER WHEN I PADDLE AND ACTS AS A **CUSHION** FOR THE OTHER PADDLERS AROUND ME."

CHOOSE ONE.

BONK

OWoooW!

THUMP

HEY!

Ⓐ

Ⓑ

IF YOU CHOOSE Ⓑ, EVERYBODY COMES OUT BETTER.

CHOONA NOW SHOWS TINA AND DOOLEY HOW TO **FORWARD PADDLE** BY KEEPING THEIR BACKS **STRAIGHT**, PADDLING ONLY ON **ONE** SIDE, AND **PULLING** THE WATER **TOWARD** THEM, WHILE CHOONA STEERS THE CANOE.

"**RIGHT ON!**" SMILES CHOONA,

"YOU GUYS ARE DOING **GREAT!**"

"BUT UNCLE CHOONA," TINA ASKS, "WHAT IF WE HAVE TO **STOP** THE CANOE? **WHAT** DO WE DO THEN?"

"WE PUT ON THE **BRAKES,**" JOKES DOOLEY.

"**HA!**" LAUGHS CHOONA. "I'LL SHOW YOU WHAT WE DO, WE **BACKPADDLE...**

"LIFT YOUR PADDLE **OUT** OF THE WATER AND TURN A LITTLE BIT **SIDEWAYS.** GOOD. NOW HOLD THE **MIDDLE** OF THE HANDLE AGAINST YOUR **HIPBONE**, PUT YOUR PADDLE **BACK** IN THE WATER, AND **PUSH** THE WATER **AWAY** FROM YOU. THAT'S RIGHT.

"OKAY, DOOLEY, CALL OUT IF YOU SEE ANYTHING UP AHEAD IN THE WATER —ROCKS, BRANCHES, TREE STUMPS, **ANYTHING**, BECAUSE...

I CAN'T SEE **THRU** YOU KIDS."

A FEW MINUTES LATER, DOOLEY SHOUTS, "**UNCLE CHOONA**, I THINK THERE'S **SOMETHING IN THE RIVER UP AHEAD!**

"A BRANCH MAYBE?

OR A...

WAUGH
WAAUGH

MOOOOOSE! "SCREAM
TINA AND DOOLEY.
"BACKPADDLE!" YELLS CHOONA,
AND ALL THREE QUICKLY **BACKPADDLE**
AS THE MOOSE LUNGES **OUT OF**
THE RIVER AND INTO THE **FOREST.**

32

"GOOD THING YOU SPOTTED THAT BRANCH, DOOLEY," LAUGHS CHOONA.

"**BRANCH**?" SAYS DOOLEY.

"YEAH, FROM A **MOOSETREE!**" LAUGHS TINA, AND THEY ALL **CRACK UP**.

"I'M GETTING HUNGRY," SAYS DOOLEY.

"ME, TOO," TINA CHIMES IN.

"OKAY, DOOLEY, KEEP A **LOOKOUT**. SOON AS YOU SPOT **CALM WATER**, WE'LL PULL INTO AN EDDY AND CATCH SOME **FISH** FOR LUNCH." UH-OH!

AROUND THE NEXT BEND DOOLEY SEES **SMOOTH WATER** AND CALLS OUT.

"OKAY, **HARD FORWARD PADDLE!**" HOLLERS CHOONA, STEERING TOWARD SHORE.

As soon as the canoe touches the beach, Choona says, "Okay, kids, stash your paddles BEHIND you. Dooley, you STEP OUT and pull the canoe up ONTO THE SAND as far as you can. Then HOLD it while TINA steps out.

"Now, both of you, pull the canoe in SOME MORE."

Then Choona steps out, and he pulls the canoe ALL THE WAY UP onto the beach.

CHOONA ASKS TINA TO GET THE
FISHING TACKLE OUT OF THE CANOE.

"HERE ARE THE **LINES** AND **HOOKS**,
UNCLE CHOONA, BUT WHERE'S THE
BAIT?"

"**UNDER THOSE ROCKS**," NODS CHOONA,
"AND IN THAT **LONG GRASS**."

HE HANDS TINA AND DOOLEY EACH A
DRAWSTRING NET BAG.

THEY FAN OUT — TINA CATCHES
GRASSHOPPERS AND **BUGS**,
AND DOOLEY AND CHOONA SCOOP UP
WORMS AND **CRAWLERS**.

CHOONA SAYS, "KIDS, THERE'S
CORNBREAD AND **TRAIL MIX** IN THE DRY
BAG AND **FRESH WATER** IN THE CANTEEN
TO HOLD YOU TILL LUNCH.

"I'M HEADING DOWNSTREAM A WAYS TO SCOUT FOR A FISHING HOLE."

BESIDE A BOULDER AND IN THE SHADE OF A BIG WILLOW TREE, CHOONA SPOTS A DEEP **KEEPER HOLE** BY THE RIVER BANK.

HOLE

RIVER FLOW

TINA AND DOOLEY JOIN CHOONA, WHO SIGNALS THEM **NOT TO TALK** AND TO MOVE **QUIETLY** SO THEY **DON'T SCARE** THE FISH. HE GIVES THEM EACH A STICK TO TIE THEIR LINES TO. THEY BAIT UP AND DROP THEIR LINES INTO THE DEEP HOLE.

RIGHT AWAY A GREAT BIG **BIG MOUTH** BASS TAKES TINA'S GRASSHOPPER.

WILLY DID IT

36

"I **GOT** ONE*!*" CROWS *TINA*. SHE JERKS THE LINE AND **SETS HER HOOK**.

"GOOD," SAYS CHOONA, "NOW **PULL** AND WIND YOUR LINE ON THE STICK."

"OH **BOY***!*" DOOLEY SHOUTS, "**LUNCH***!*"

37

"I'LL TAKE FIRST TURN AT CLEANING FISH," SAYS CHOONA AS THEY WALK BACK TO THE CANOE, "YOU KIDS GATHER WOOD AND GET A FIRE GOING!"

HIGH-WATER DRY WOOD

DOOLEY SCRAPES OUT A PIT WITH A WEDGE-SHAPED STONE, AND TINA BRINGS IN 4 ROCKS FOR THE FRY PAN TO SIT ON.

DOOLEY WATCHES THE FIRE AS IT DIES DOWN TO HOT COALS (PERFECT FOR COOKING).

CHOONA CLEANS THE FISH AND HANGS IT FROM A BRANCH IN A BURLAP BAG. THEN HE GATHERS WATERCRESS AND MINER'S LETTUCE BY A SIDE STREAM, WHILE TINA PICKS WILD BLACKBERRIES FOR DESSERT.

CHOONA COOKS UP A SWELL MEAL.
WHILE THEY'RE EATING, DOOLEY SAYS
"LOOK!" AND THEY ALL LOOK TOWARD
THE RIVER.

A FISH HAWK SWOOPS LOW OVER THE
WATER AND **GRABS** A **BIG FISH** IN ITS
CLAWS.

"NICE CATCH!" SHOUTS DOOLEY.

"WATCH," CHOONA WHISPERS, NODDING
AT THE SKY.

HIGH OVERHEAD, A HOVERING EAGLE
FOLDS ITS WINGS, DROPS **LIKE A ROCK**
IN A FAST DIVE, AND ...

...SNATCHES THE FISH FROM THE HAWK.

"OH WOW!" GASPS TINA.
TUMBLING IN THE AIR, THE HAWK
RIGHTS ITSELF AND CHASES AFTER

THE EAGLE, SHRIEKING, "SHREEE! CHREEEE!"

BUT THE EAGLE CLIMBS HIGHER AND HIGHER, LEAVING THE SMALLER BIRD BEHIND.

THE HAWK BREAKS OFF THE CHASE, DROPS BACK DOWN TO THE RIVER, AND CIRCLES UP AND DOWNSTREAM JUST OVER THE WATER.

SWOOOSH! HE CATCHES A SECOND FISH AND, FLYING BELOW THE TREETOPS, CARRIES IT BACK TO HIS NEST.

"PRETTY GOOD SHOW," SAYS CHOONA. "YOU KIDS LEARN ANYTHING FROM THAT HAWK?"

"I THINK THAT HAWK WAS DUMB! HE SHOULD'VE GOT HIS FISH BACK...

... FROM THE EAGLE," SAYS DOOLEY, POPPING ANOTHER BLACKBERRY INTO HIS MOUTH.

"BUT, UNCLE CHOONA," ASKS TINA, "ISN'T THAT EAGLE A **LOT STRONGER** THAN THE FISH HAWK?"

"YES," CHOONA ANSWERS, "AND THE HAWK **KNOWS** THAT."

"OH," SAYS DOOLEY, "**THAT'S** WHY HE CAUGHT THE SECOND FISH — HE GOT TO EAT **WITHOUT** GETTING **HURT.**

"GUESS HE'S **NOT** SO DUMB AFTER ALL."

"MAYBE SO," SAYS CHOONA, SETTING HIS EMPTY BOWL ASIDE AND LYING BACK ON THE WARM SAND.

HE LOOKS AT THE SUNLIGHT COMING THRU THE TREES AND SEES HIS **GRANDFATHER'S FACE** IN THE CLOUDS,

SMILING DOWN AT HIM.

CHOONA GETS UP, GRABS THE FRY PAN, THROWS IN A HANDFUL OF SAND, AND WALKS DOWN TO THE RIVER. HE SCOOPS UP SOME WATER AND HEADS BACK UP TO THE FIRE PIT.

SCOURING OUT THE PAN, CHOONA **POURS** THE SANDY **WATER ONTO THE COALS** AND SAYS, "YOU KIDS DO THE SAME WITH THE DISHES."

AFTER TINA AND DOOLEY HAVE POURED THEIR SANDY WATER ON THE COALS, CHOONA **BURIES**...

...THE FIRE PIT   8 FINGERS DEEP
WITH SAND.

"LET'S PICK UP ANY LITTER,"
SAYS CHOONA HOLDING A TRASH BAG,
"AND LEAVE THIS PLACE **CLEANER**
THAN WHEN WE FOUND IT.

"YOU KIDS DID A **GREAT** JOB. NOW
LET'S LOAD UP, AND I'LL SHOW YOU HOW
TO STEER THE CANOE."

HE PUSHES THE CANOE OFF INTO THE
EDDY, CLIMBS IN THE **BACK**,

AND ASKS TINA AND DOOLEY TO WADE
IN AND **HOLD THE FRONT** STEADY.

"THIS WAY," CHOONA SAYS,

"IT'S EASIER FOR YOU KIDS TO WATCH THAN SITTING IN THE CANOE.

"HERE'S HOW TO STEER — REMEMBER ONLY THE PERSON IN BACK STEERS — EVERYONE IN FRONT JUST PADDLES.

"IT DOESN'T MATTER WHETHER YOU STEER ON THE RIGHT OR LEFT SIDE OF THE CANOE — JUST CHOOSE ONE SIDE AND STAY WITH IT — SO YOU DON'T WEAR YOURSELF OUT SWITCHING SIDES. HOLD YOUR PADDLE INTO THE WATER AT AN ANGLE.

SPLASH

WILLY DID IT

"WHEN YOU WANT TO GO STRAIGHT, KEEP THE BLADE IN LINE WITH THE CANOE — AND THE CANOE WILL GO STRAIGHT...

"WHEN YOU WANT TO GO **RIGHT**, TURN THE **BACK** OF YOUR BLADE **RIGHT**—AND THE **CANOE** WILL GO TO THE **RIGHT**. **WHEN YOU WANT TO GO LEFT**, TURN THE **BACK** OF YOUR BLADE **LEFT**—AND THE **CANOE** WILL GO TO THE **LEFT**."

"BUT, UNCLE CHOONA, WHAT DO YOU DO IF YOU'RE ALL BY YOURSELF?" ASKS DOOLEY.

"GOOD QUESTION," SAYS CHOONA, "I'LL **SHOW** YOU. WHEN YOU'RE BY YOURSELF, YOU NEED TO **PADDLE**

AND *STEER* AT THE *SAME* TIME.

"SAY YOU'RE STEERING ON THE *RIGHT.* IF YOU JUST PADDLE ALONG, YOUR CANOE WILL START TO GO *LEFT* IN A *CIRCLE.* TO KEEP GOING *STRAIGHT,* HERE'S WHAT YOU DO.

"WITH EACH STROKE OF YOUR PADDLE, YOU *PULL* **BACK,** *TURN* THE BLADE, AND *PUSH* **AWAY** — THIS MAKES AN **L** IN THE WATER, SO WE CALL IT AN *L-STROKE...*

PULL

START THE LETTER **L**

TURN

PUSH AWAY
FINISH THE LETTER **L**

WILY DID IT

"BY *PUSHING AWAY* AT THE END OF EACH STROKE, YOU KEEP YOUR CANOE GOING **STRAIGHT.** THIS WORKS WHETHER YOU STEER ON THE **RIGHT** OR THE **LEFT** SIDE. **PULL BACK, TURN, PUSH AWAY** KEEPS YOU GOING **STRAIGHT.**

"AS SOON AS YOU GET SOME

FLAP FLAP

FLAP FLAP

SPEED UP, YOU CAN STEER WITH YOUR PADDLE BLADE *LIKE BEFORE* —JUST AS IF YOU HAD **PADDLERS** IN **FRONT.**

"WE HAVE A **LONG** STRETCH OF **SMOOTH RIVER** AHEAD OF US, SO WHICH ONE OF YOU WOULD LIKE TO STEER **FIRST** ?"

"ME! ME! ME! ME!" SHOUT TINA AND

DOOLEY TOGETHER.

CHOONA HOPS OUT OF THE CANOE, WADES ASHORE, AND PICKS UP A TWIG. HE SNAPS IT INTO **2 PIECES** AND HOLDS THEM IN HIS FIST WITH **JUST THE ENDS** STICKING UP.

"DRAW—LONG ONE GOES **FIRST.**"

"**YEA!** "SAYS TINA, "I GO **FIRST!**"

THEY LOAD THE CANOE—TINA CLIMBS IN **BACK** TO **STEER** CHOONA SITS IN THE **MIDDLE**, AND DOOLEY SITS UP **FRONT.**

THE CANOE MOVES AWAY FROM THE BEACH AND **ZIG-ZAGS** DOWN THE RIVER AS TINA TRIES TO STEER IT.

WHEN YOU GET THE **HANG** OF IT," CHOONA TELLS HER, "IT'S AS EASY AS **BREATHING.**"

"I THINK I'M CATCHING ON," TINA SAYS, AND THE CANOE STARTS TO **SMOOTH** OUT AND GLIDE **STRAIGHT** DOWNSTREAM.

AROUND THE NEXT BEND, THEY SPOT A **MAMA BLACK BEAR** FISHING WHILE HER **2 CUBS** PLAY ON THE SHORE.

"**FREEZE**," WHISPERS CHOONA.

HE MOTIONS TO TINA TO **KEEP STEERING**, AS HE **QUIET PADDLES** THE CANOE **PAST** THE BEARS.

WHEN THEY ARE **WELL BEYOND** THE BEARS, CHOONA SAYS, "MAMA BEARS **PROTECT** THEIR CUBS. IT'S GOOD THE WIND WAS BLOWING **FROM** THEM **TOWARD** US. IF MAMA BEAR HAD **GOT OUR SCENT** AND THOUGHT HER CUBS WERE IN **DANGER**, NO TELLING WHAT SHE MIGHT HAVE DONE. BEARS **DON'T SEE** TOO WELL, BUT THEY CAN **SMELL** THINGS **A MILE** AWAY."

"UNCLE CHOONA," ASKS DOOLEY, "WILL YOU TEACH US HOW TO **PADDLE QUIETLY** LIKE YOU JUST DID?"

"SURE," SAYS CHOONA, "TOMORROW AFTER BREAKFAST. OKAY, TINA, NOW IT'S...

...DOOLEY'S TURN. SO LET'S
PADDLE ASHORE, STRETCH OUR LEGS,
AND PICK SOME BLACKBERRIES."

THEY PUT IN AT THE NEXT EDDY,
AND AS THEY ALL GET OUT, DOOLEY
SAYS, "I'LL PULL THE CANOE **UP ON
THE BEACH** AND CATCH UP WITH YOU."

WHILE TINA, DOOLEY, AND CHOONA
ARE PICKING BLACKBERRIES, THE 2
BEAR CUBS COME SCAMPERING ALONG THE
SHORE. THEY LIFT THEIR NOSES AND SNIFF.

SMELLING THE
ODOR OF FISH,
THEY RUN OVER TO THE CANOE TO FIND
OUT WHERE IT'S COMING FROM.
SCRATCH! BUMP! **THUD!** RIP! **TEAR!**

AND THE CUBS ARE IN THE FOOD BAG, LICKING THE FRY PAN AND THE BOWLS.

DOOLEY ONLY PULLED THE CANOE HALFWAY UP ON THE BEACH, LEAVING THE OTHER HALF IN THE WATER.

THE ROLLICKING CUBS ROCK AND ROLL THE CANOE UNTIL, BEFORE THEY KNOW IT, THE CANOE SLIDES OFF THE BEACH AND QUIETLY INTO THE RIVER.

THE CANOE DRIFTS **OUT** OF THE **EDDY** AND **INTO THE MAIN CURRENT.** WHEN IT STARTS TO **SPIN AROUND,** THE CUBS LOOK UP. ONE TRIES TO **CLIMB OUT** AND **ALMOST TIPS** THE CANOE OVER, BUT WHEN HE SEES IT'S **ALL WATER** AND **NO LAND,** HE BEGINS TO BAWL AND HIS SISTER JOINS IN — "**EOWWRRR OUGGH!**"

MAMA BEAR **STOPS** FISHING, LOOKS UP, AND **HEARS** HER CUBS CRYING. **OORAWARGHH!** SHE GROWLS. LUNGING DOWNSTREAM, SHE TAKES OFF AT A **FULL RUN**

AFTER THE **CRYING CUB CANOE.**

"I THINK I JUST SAW A **BEAR** RUN BY," SAYS DOOLEY.

"OH YEAH, UH-HUH, SURE," MUMBLES TINA WITH HER MOUTH FULL OF BLACKBERRIES.

"LET'S LOOK," SAYS CHOONA.

"**HEY!** THE CANOE IS **GONE!**" SHOUTS DOOLEY, AND THEY ALL RUN **DOWN THE SHORE.**

"**I SEE IT!**" YELLS TINA, AND IT'S FULL OF **BEARS!**"

"THERE'S MAMA BEAR RUNNING AHEAD OF US," SAYS DOOLEY.

CHOONA PUTS HIS HANDS ON TINA AND DOOLEY'S SHOULDER. "WE MUST BE **QUIET** AND **NOT PASS** HER UP,"

HE WHISPERS.

MAMA BEAR IS TOO WORRIED ABOUT HER CUBS TO BOTHER WITH THE PEOPLE BEHIND HER.

EEEARROWWOOGH! CRY THE CUBS FROM THE CANOE

OOoRAWRRGHH?! BELLOWS MAMA BACK.

A WAYS DOWNSTREAM THE CANOE BUMPS INTO A FALLEN TREE, SPINS AROUND, AND WEDGES AGAINST THE TREE'S TRUNK. THE CUBS QUICKLY CLIMB ONTO THE TREE AND SCAMPER ASHORE.

TINA, DOOLEY, AND CHOONA WATCH FROM A DISTANCE AS MAMA LICKS HER CUBS AND GROWLS AT THEM FOR WANDERING OFF TO JOIN THE NAVY.

WHEN THE BEARS ARE GONE, CHOONA **WALKS** OUT ON THE FALLEN TREE TRUNK TO THE CANOE, **DROPS** TO HIS **STOMACH**, AND REACHES IN FOR A **THROWBAG**.

PULLING OUT THE ROPE, HE TIES **ONE END** TO THE **CANOE**, THEN GETS UP AND **RUNS ASHORE** WITH THE **OTHER** END. HE GIVES THE ROPE A **WRAP** AROUND A **SMALL TREE** AND ASKS TINA AND DOOLEY TO **PULL** FROM THE **SHORE** WHILE HE WADES OUT TO **PULL** FROM THE **RIVER.** TOGETHER...

. . . THEY **WORK** THE CANOE **FREE** AND PULL IT UP ONTO THE SHORE.

"NOT TOO BAD," CHOONA SAYS, RELIEVED, "IT'S A MESS, BUT NOTHING'S LOST."

"THEY **BEAR**-LY TOUCHED IT!" JOKES DOOLEY, AND THEY ALL CRACK UP.

"BOY, WHAT IF THE CUBS HAD MADE IT **ALL THE WAY** TO RIVER RATS' ROOST?" LAUGHS TINA. "I CAN JUST SEE DAD'S FACE — **OH NO!** THE KIDS HAVE TURNED INTO **BEARS!**"

AND THEY ALL CRACK UP SOME MORE.

THEY STRAIGHTEN UP THE CANOE AND WASH OUT THE FRY PAN AND COOKWARE WITH **SOAP** AND **WATER** AND ELBOW GREASE, AND WHEN IT'S LOOKING **GOOD**, THEY SHOVE OFF.

DOOLEY TAKES HIS TURN AT STEERING, WHILE TINA AND CHOONA PADDLE. ONCE AGAIN THE CANOE **ZIG-ZAGS** DOWNRIVER UNTIL DOOLEY GETS THE **HANG** OF IT.

WHEN THE SUN IS 3 HANDS FROM SETTING, CHOONA SAYS, "**LISTEN**, WHAT DO YOU **HEAR**?"

"SOUNDS LIKE A **TRAIN**," SAYS TINA.

"ON THE **RIVER**?" ASKS DOOLEY.

WHOOSH

"NO," SAYS TINA, LEANING FORWARD, "IT MUST BE A **WATERFALL.**"

"RIGHT," SAYS CHOONA. "DOOLEY, STEER ASHORE, INTO THAT **EDDY** ON THE **RIGHT...**

AND WE'LL **MAKE CAMP** FOR THE NIGHT." THEY PULL THE CANOE ONTO THE BEACH, UNLOAD THEIR GEAR, AND CARRY IT INTO THE WOODS.

CHOONA LEADS TINA AND DOOLEY INTO A **CLEARING.**

"GRANDFATHER AND I USED TO CAMP HERE," HE SAYS, STOPPING BY AN OLD **FIRE RING.**

AFTER THEY PUT THEIR STUFF DOWN, CHOONA SAYS, "OKAY, NOW LET'S GO BACK AND **GET THE CANOE.** THAT WAY WE'LL HAVE IT HERE TO CARRY DOWN THE TRAIL **PAST THE FALLS.**"

"**HEY,**" GRINS DOOLEY, "INSTEAD OF GOING **AROUND,** WHY DON'T WE JUST GO **DOWN THE FALLS?**"

"I'LL **TELL** YOU WHY..." EXPLAINS CHOONA.

THEY BRING BACK THE CANOE, SET UP CAMP, AND GET A **CAMPFIRE** GOING.

CHOONA STRETCHES THE **RAIN TARP**
BETWEEN TWO TREES
AND SHOWS THE
KIDS HOW TO
MAKE SOFT

WHERE YOU WANT TO
TIE THE TARP - **PUT** IN
A **ROCK**, TIE THE ROPE
TIGHT - TARP STAYS AND
WON'T BLOW AWAY.

TARP

PINE NEEDLE BEDS TO PUT THEIR
SLEEPING BAGS ON.

FALLEN
PINE NEEDLES

DOOLEY DIGS A DITCH
3 FINGERS DEEP AROUND
THE EDGE OF THE TARP IN
CASE OF RAIN—TO **DRAIN** THE **WATER**
AWAY.

"I'LL STAY BEHIND TO GATHER
MORE WOOD AND WATCH THE FIRE,"
SAYS TINA, "WHILE YOU GUYS GET WHAT
WE NEED FOR DINNER."

"GREAT," SAYS CHOONA, PICKING
UP THE **CANTEEN** AND A COUPLE OF **NET**
BAGS." C'MON, DOOLEY, LET'S GO

SEE WHAT WE CAN FIND."

ON THE **NORTH** SIDE OF THE HILL THEY COME UPON THE **DARK RED** BRANCHES OF THE **MANZANITA** BUSH.

CHOONA GATHERS A HANDFUL OF BERRIES AND, PUTTING THEM IN DOOLEY'S NET BAG, SAYS,

"PICK ONLY THE **BROWN** BERRIES, **NOT** THE **GREEN** ONES." HE POPS A FEW INTO HIS MOUTH. "MMM, SWEET. TRY SOME."

"**HEYYY**," SAYS DOOLEY, THEY TASTE LIKE LITTLE APPLES."

"YES," REPLIES CHOONA, "AND THEY MAKE GREAT **APPLE PIE** OR **APPLESAUCE** FOR DESSERT."

WHILE DOOLEY FILLS HIS NET BAG WITH **RIPE BERRIES**, CHOONA . . .

STARTS OFF DOWNHILL TOWARD A **SIDE STREAM**. "I'M GOING FOR WATER AND TO PICK SOME **GREENS**. I'LL BE RIGHT BACK."

HE FILLS THE CANTEEN WHERE THE CRYSTAL-CLEAR WATER BUBBLES OUT OF THE ROCK. NEXT HE SLIDES HIS HAND DOWN TO THE BOTTOM OF THE **CATTAILS** GROWING **IN THE WATER** NEARBY AND PULLS THEM UP. HE **CUTS OFF THE GREEN** TOPS AND **PUTS THE WHITE LOWER STALKS** INTO HIS NET BAG, ALONG WITH A FEW HANDFULS OF **WILD CLOVER** FOR A SALAD.

BY THE TIME CHOONA AND
DOOLEY GET BACK TO CAMP, TINA
HAS GATHERED A GOOD SUPPLY OF
DEAD BRANCHES TO KEEP THE FIRE
GOING AND HAS LAID OUT THE BOWLS
AND COOKWARE FOR DINNER.

CHOONA SETS
TO WORK
MAKING **POLENTA.**
FIRST HE PUTS A POT OF WATER
ON TO BOIL. NEXT HE MIXES
CORN MEAL AND **SEASONING** AND
STIRS IN SOME COLD **WATER.**

THEN, WHEN THE POT OF WATER
STARTS TO BOIL, HE
SLOWLY POURS IN THE CORN MEAL
MIX AND **KEEPS STIRRING** SO THE
BOTTOM **WON'T BURN.**

TINA MAKES THE **SALAD—**

SHE CUTS UP THE **CATTAIL STALKS**, ADDS THE **CLOVER**, AND TOSSES IT ALL UP IN A BOWL WITH SOME **SALAD DRESSING** CHOONA BROUGHT ALONG.

"HOW ABOUT **MANZANITA APPLE PIE** FOR DESSERT?" SAYS CHOONA.

"HUH?" ASKS TINA.

"YEAH," SAYS DOOLEY, "THEY'RE REALLY **GOOD!**"

DOOLEY GRINDS HALF A BAG OF BERRIES ON A **FLAT ROCK** TO MAKE THE PIE **FILLING**, WHILE CHOONA MIXES FLOUR AND WATER TO MAKE THE **CRUST**. THEN THEY SET THE PIE ON A **BED** OF **COALS** AND **COVER** IT WITH A BOWL TO **BAKE**.

GOOD SMELL →
RED HOT COALS IN PIT →
BOWL
AIR IN, SO COALS STAY HOT.
← PIE INSIDE UNDER BOWL.
← LITTLE ROCK TILTS BOWL, OVEN.

CHOONA MIX FOR SALADS VINEGAR OLIVE OIL SPICES

"UNCLE CHOONA," SAYS DOOLEY, HELPING HIMSELF TO SECONDS, "I REALLY LIKE THE **WILD FOODS** WE'VE BEEN EATING."

"ME, TOO," AGREES TINA. "BUT HOW DO YOU KNOW WHICH PLANTS ARE **GOOD TO EAT**?"

"**GRANDMOTHER** TAUGHT ME," REPLIES CHOONA. "OUR PEOPLE HAVE KNOWN THESE THINGS FOR AS LONG AS **ANYONE** CAN REMEMBER."

"WHAT A GREAT MEAL," SIGHS TINA, POLISHING OFF HER **THIRD** PIECE OF MANZANITA PIE.

"SOME FOLKS DON'T KNOW WHAT THEY'RE MISSING," SMILES CHOONA. HE PUTS ANOTHER BRANCH ON THE FIRE, LEANS BACK, AND LOOKS UP AT THE NIGHT SKY FULL OF STARS SO CLOSE...

...THAT YOU CAN ALMOST *TOUCH* THEM.

"SO," CHOONA ASKS, "WHAT DID WE **LEARN** TODAY FROM THE **LONG PERSON**?"

"THAT WE MUST **SHARE** THE RIVER WITH THE **BEARS**," LAUGHS TINA.

"RIGHT," SAYS DOOLEY, "AND

NEXT TIME I'LL PULL THE CANOE
ALL THE WAY UP SO WE DON'T HAVE
TO SHARE IT WITH THE BEARS, JUST
THE RIVER."

"AND WHAT ELSE?" ASKS CHOONA.

"THAT WE MUST ALWAYS BE READY
FOR SURPRISES—LIKE THE
MOOSE," SAYS DOOLEY.

"AND THE FISH HAWK TAUGHT US
WHEN TO TURN FROM TROUBLE AND
TAKE CARE OF OURSELVES," ADDS
TINA.

"YOU HAVE LEARNED SOME GOOD
THINGS TODAY," CHOONA SMILES.

"THE LONG PERSON SPEAKS TO US,
BUT NOT IN WORDS — HE GIVES US
MANY THOUGHTS TO HELP US ON THE
RIVER OF LIFE."

CHOONA GETS UP AND ...

...THROWS ANOTHER BRANCH ON THE FIRE.
TINA AND DOOLEY GRAB A *FLASHLIGHT*
AND GO DOWN TO THE RIVER FOR
WATER TO WASH THE DISHES.

WHILE THEY'RE GONE, CHOONA
WIPES THE FRY PAN CLEAN, POURS
IN A LITTLE **OIL** AND A COUPLE
HANDFULS OF **POPCORN KERNELS**,
COVERS IT WITH A **STEEL BOWL**,
AND SETS IT BACK ON THE FIRE.

BOWL FITS INSIDE
FRY PAN
POP DING
← GOOD SMELL
FRY PAN ON
TOP OF ROCKS
DING
POP
RED HOT
COALS
← ROCKS

IN NO TIME
THE POPCORN
STARTS POPPING
AGAINST THE BOWL, AS CHOONA
SHAKES THE FRY PAN BACK AND FORTH
OVER THE COALS. HE **KEEPS** ON **SHAKING**
UNTIL HE HEARS THE **LAST KERNEL**
POP, JUST AS TINA AND DOOLEY
GET BACK TO CAMP.

70

CHOONA TAKES THE PAN AND BOWL OFF THE FIRE, AND QUICKLY **FLIPS** THEM **UPSIDE DOWN** — CLANG! HE LIFTS OFF THE FRY PAN — AND THERE'S A HOT BOWL FULL OF POPCORN. "**WOW!** NEAT TRICK, UNCLE CHOONA," SAY THE KIDS.

POP

YAHHHH!

POP

POP

LIFT OFF

CAUTION HOT BOWL! LET COOL

CHOONA REACHES INTO THE DRY BAG, GETS OUT THE **POPCORN SEASONING**, SPRINKLES SOME ON, AND SAYS, "DIG IN."

WHILE THEY MUNCH POPCORN, CHOONA LEANS AGAINST THE TREE AND PLAYS HIS **FLUTE** TO THE STARS.

BEFORE LONG, THE COALS DIE DOWN TO A FAINT GLOW. CHOONA **POURS** SOME **WATER** ON THEM AND **COVERS** THEM WITH **EARTH** — SO NO HOT SPARK CAN START A **FOREST FIRE.**

HE PULLS THE DRY BAG WITH ALL THEIR FOOD ALL THE WAY UP TO THE **HIGHEST** BRANCH — SO THE BEARS WON'T GET IT — AND TIES IT OFF FOR THE NIGHT.

OUR SLEEPY-EYED CAMPERS CRAWL INTO THEIR SLEEPING BAGS AND **SOON** FALL FAST ASLEEP.

AS THE SUN PEEKS OVER THE MOUNTAINTOPS, TINA AND DOOLEY WAKE UP TO THE SMELL OF **PANCAKES.**

"G'MORNING, UNCLE CHOONA," THE KIDS SAY SLEEPILY. "MMMMM, BOY, THAT SMELLS GOOD." AND THEY HIKE OFF TO THE SIDE STREAM TO SPLASH SOME COLD WATER ON THEIR FACES.

WHEN THEY COME BACK, CHOONA HANDS THEM EACH A MUG OF HOT **MANZANITA BERRY TEA.**

"THERE'S PLENTY OF **PANCAKES** AND **MAPLE SYRUP** BY THE FIRE. HELP YOURSELVES."

AFTER A HEARTY BREAKFAST, THEY WASH UP AND BREAK CAMP,

IT'S DOWN!

WHUMP

MAKING SURE AGAIN THAT THEIR FIRE
IS **SOAKED** AND **COVERED.**

"UNCLE CHOONA, CAN I HELP CARRY
THE **CANOE**?" ASKS TINA.

"I CAN CARRY THE **DRY BAG,**"
SAYS DOOLEY.

"SURE," SAYS CHOONA, AND THEY
SET OFF DOWN THE TRAIL AROUND
THE FALLS.

"WHAT WE'RE DOING IS CALLED
A **PORTAGE,**" EXPLAINS CHOONA.

"A **PARTRIDGE**?" ASKS DOOLEY.

"NO SILLY," TEASES TINA, "THAT'S
A BIRD. **PORRIDGE!**"

"OH **MUSH!**" GRINS DOOLEY.

"*MUSH ON!*" SMILES CHOONA, AND THEY ALL LAUGH.

JUST BELOW THE FALLS, TINA AND DOOLEY WADE IN AND HOLD THE CANOE WHILE CHOONA SHOWS THEM HOW TO **QUIET PADDLE.**

"*REMEMBER HOW TO DO THE* **L-STROKE**?" ASKS CHOONA.

"SURE, WE DO," SAY TINA AND DOOLEY.

"WELL, TO QUIET PADDLE, YOU MUST USE A **SPECIAL** L-STROKE. THE BLADE OF YOUR PADDLE MUST **NEVER LEAVE THE WATER.** FIRST, YOU **SLIDE** YOUR PADDLE BLADE...

...QUIETLY **ALL THE WAY** INTO THE WATER **IN LINE** WITH THE **CANOE.**

BIRDS EYE VIEW

BLADE DOWN ALL THE WAY

BLADE IN LINE WITH CANOE

FROGS EYE VIEW

"WATCH CAREFULLY... Ⓐ WITH YOUR **TOP** HAND YOU **TURN** AND Ⓑ WITH YOUR **BOTTOM** HAND YOU **PULL BACK.** THEN Ⓒ WITH YOUR **TOP HAND TURN** AND Ⓓ WITH YOUR **BOTTOM** HAND **PUSH AWAY.** NOW Ⓔ **QUIETLY SLICE FORWARD**... AND BEGIN AGAIN.

Ⓐ SLICE FORWARD   TURN   Willy DID IT

UNDERWATER L-STROKE   QUIETLY!   TURN Ⓒ

PUSH Ⓓ   Ⓔ SLICE FORWARD

BLADE UNDERWATER THE WHOLE TIME
WATER LINE

SLICE FORWARD TURN Ⓐ PULL BACK Ⓑ QUIETLY! Ⓒ TURN Ⓓ PUSH Ⓔ SLICE FORWARD

"**QUIET PADDLING**," CHOONA CONTINUES, "IS **NOT AS FAST** AS **NORMAL** PADDLING. WE QUIET PADDLE TO GET **SAFELY PAST** ANIMALS—OR PEOPLE—ON SHORE, SO WE **DON'T DISTURB** THEM."

"LIKE MAMA BEAR?" DOOLEY ASKS, CLIMBING ABOARD.

"OR FISHERMEN ON THE BANK?" ADDS TINA, AS SHE GETS IN FRONT.

"RIGHT," SAYS CHOONA. "YOU KIDS CAN QUIET PADDLE FROM **WHERE YOU SIT**—ONLY YOU **DON'T PUSH AWAY**. JUST PADDLE WITH YOUR BLADE **ALL THE WAY** IN THE WATER. **SLIDE** YOUR PADDLE IN, **TURN**, **PULL BACK**,

TURN, *SLICE FORWARD*, TURN, AND
PULL BACK AGAIN—AS *QUIETLY*
AS YOU CAN—AND I'LL **STEER** FROM
BACK HERE."

"**WOW!** THIS IS NEAT," LAUGHS
DOOLEY, AND WITH A **RAAWWCKK!**
A STARTLED **GREAT BLUE HERON**
TAKES WING IN FRONT OF THEM.

"OOPS," DOOLEY WHISPERS,
"GUESS I NEED TO BE AS QUIET AS
MY **PADDLE.**"

AS THE HERON LANDS DOWNRIVER

ON A ROCK OUTCROP,
CHOONA STEERS
THE CANOE INTO THE **MAIN CURRENT.**

"MAYBE SO. NOW LET'S **NORMAL**
PADDLE SO WE CAN GET TO A FISHING
HOLE I KNOW BEFORE NOON."

THEY PICK UP THE PACE, AND THE
CANOE PLANES SMOOTHLY OVER THE
WATER.

WHERE THE RIVER IS **NARROW,** THE
CURRENT IS **SWIFT,** AND CARRIES
THEM QUICKLY. BUT WHERE IT
GROWS **WIDER,** THE RIVER **SLOWS DOWN.**

SUDDENLY THEY COME TO A FORK
IN THE RIVER, WHERE IT SPLITS AND
FLOWS LEFT AND RIGHT AROUND...

...WHAT SEEMS LIKE AN ISLAND.

"THE RIVER'S SO **WIDE**, AND THE CURRENT'S SO **SLOW**, IT'S HARD TO TELL WHICH WAY TO GO," SAYS TINA, LOOKING AHEAD.

"WHICH WAY, UNCLE CHOONA?" ASKS DOOLEY.

"YOU KIDS CHOOSE," SAYS CHOONA. TINA AND DOOLEY TALK IT OVER AND DECIDE TO GO **LEFT**.

CHOONA STEERS LEFT AND THE KIDS PADDLE. AFTER A WAYS, THE RIVER **BENDS** AND THE BUSHES AND TREES SEEM TO BE **GETTING CLOSER** TOGETHER.

"BRANCHES AHEAD!" TINA CALLS OUT.
"LOOKS LIKE A DEAD END,"
GROANS DOOLEY.

"I THINK WE CHOSE THE WRONG
WAY," SIGHS TINA.

"DOOLEY, STOP AND PUT YOUR
PADDLE UP. TINA, BACKPADDLE,"
SAYS CHOONA, TURNING THE CANOE
AROUND WITH A SWEEP STROKE.

THE CANOE SCRAPES OVER THE TIPS
OF DEAD BRANCHES AND POINTS BACK
UPRIVER.

"FORWARD PADDLE," CALLS CHOONA.

81

AS THEY PADDLE BACK TO THE FORK IN THE RIVER, CHOONA BREAKS THE SILENCE. "SOMETIMES WE CHOOSE THE WRONG WAY. WHEN THE CURRENT IS **SLOW**, THE RIVER LETS US **TURN AROUND** AND **TRY AGAIN.**

"WHEN IT'S **FAST** AND WE **CAN'T SEE** FAR AHEAD, IT'S BEST TO PADDLE **ASHORE**, WALK ALONG THE RIVER, AND **SCOUT** IT OUT."

THEY COME AROUND THE TIP OF THE ISLAND AND TURN DOWNRIVER.

WHEN THE SUN IS **2** FINGERS FROM NOON, THEY REACH CHOONA'S FISHING HOLE.

AFTER A COOL SWIM IN THE EDDY, THEY DRY OFF IN THE SUN AND GO FISHING.

CHOONA AND DOOLEY CATCH A COUPLE OF **LUNKER TROUT**, WHICH THEY COOK UP WITH A POT OF **WILD RICE**, AND A **MEADOW SWEET** SALAD ON THE SIDE.

TINA MAKES THEM A SWELL JUICE DRINK FROM FRESH-PICKED **WILD GRAPES** AND SPRING WATER.

CHOONA PULLS 3 **NET HAMMOCKS** OUT OF THE DRY BAG. THEY EACH FIND TREES TO TIE THEM BETWEEN, AND THEY SETTLE IN FOR A NICE NAP.

A **BAND** OF BANDIT **SCRUB JAYS**, LOOKING FOR SOMETHING TO EAT, **KKRKRKRKKRUTTS** THEM AWAKE.

"OKAY, KIDS," SAYS CHOONA AFTER THEY BREAK CAMP AND LOAD THE CANOE, "I WANT TO SHOW YOU **2 PADDLE STROKES** YOU CAN USE TO HELP ME STEER THRU **WHITEWATER."**

TINA AND DOOLEY AGAIN HOLD THE FRONT OF THE CANOE AS CHOONA GETS INTO THE MIDDLE.

"SAY THERE'S A **BOULDER** ON THE **RIGHT** AND WE WANT TO MOVE **AWAY** FROM IT SO WE CAN STEER **THRU THE TONGUE** — THE FLOW OF SMOOTH WATER **BETWEEN THE** BOULDERS.

"BUT THE **STRONG CURRENT**

IS FORCING US **TOWARD** THE **BOULDER.**
YOU CAN HELP ME STEER BY USING
A **PRY** STROKE ON THE **RIGHT** SIDE—
PUSHING **AWAY** FROM THE CANOE

LIKE SO...   OR A **DRAW**

TOP HAND PULLS

Ⓐ

BOULDER

KEEP
BACK
STRAIGHT

LEAN
THE
CANOE

CANOE
MOVES AWAY
FROM
BOULDER

PUSH AWAY

STROKE ON THE
LEFT SIDE—
PULLING
TOWARD THE

CANOE LIKE SO...

Ⓑ

KEEP
BACK
STRAIGHT
AND LEAN THE
CANOE

TOP HAND
PUSHES

BOTTOM
HAND
PULLS

CANOE
MOVES
AWAY FROM
BOULDER

WHEN YOU Ⓐ **PRY**
(**PUSH AWAY**),
BRACE YOUR
PADDLE WITH
YOUR **TOP** HAND
AND **PUSH AWAY** FROM THE CANOE
WITH YOUR **BOTTOM** HAND **CLOSE**
TO THE **BLADE.** BUT WHEN YOU
Ⓑ **DRAW** (**PULL TOWARD**), **BRACE**...

... YOUR PADDLE WITH YOUR **TOP** HAND AND **PULL TOWARD** THE CANOE WITH YOUR **BOTTOM** HAND **CLOSE** TO THE **BLADE**.

"C'MON, HOP IN, **GRAB** YOUR PADDLES, AND LET'S TRY IT," SAYS CHOONA. "THIS TIME, I'LL STAY IN THE **MIDDLE**.

"**BACKPADDLE**," CHOONA CALLS OUT, AND WHEN THE CANOE IS IN LINE WITH THE MAIN CURRENT,

"NOW, **HARD** FORWARD **PADDLE!**" AND THE CANOE SURGES DOWNRIVER.

WITH DOOLEY IN **FRONT** AND TINA IN THE **BACK**, THEY HEAD INTO A SMOOTH STRETCH OF WATER.

"DOOLEY, **DRAW LEFT**," CHOONA CALLS, PUTTING HIS PADDLE **UP**.

TINA, **DRAW RIGHT**,"  AND THE CANOE QUICKLY TURNS TO THE **LEFT.**

"OKAY, NOW, DOOLEY, **PRY LEFT.** TINA, **PRY RIGHT,**" AND THE CANOE TURNS BACK TO THE **RIGHT.** Ⓑ

"THIS IS **FUN!**" LAUGHS DOOLEY. "HEY, WE'RE GOING IN **CIRCLES,**" TINA CHIMES IN.

"**LISTEN,**" WHISPERS CHOONA.

"WHAT'S THAT, UP AHEAD?" ASKS TINA, STRAINING TO HEAR.

"SOUNDS LIKE MARBLES IN A JAR," GRINS DOOLEY.

"YES," SAYS CHOONA, "THE RIVER 'AKES THAT SOUND WHEN IT RUNS...

...*SHALLOW* OVER SMALLER ROCKS. "THERE'S A **BIG BEND** UP AHEAD. WE NEED TO PUT ASHORE AND GO SCOUT IT."

THEY *BEACH* THE CANOE AND HIKE UP TO THE TOP OF A HILL *OVERLOOKING* THE **BEND.**

AS THEY GAZE DOWN ON THE SWIRLING **WHITEWATER,** CHOONA ASKS,

"DO YOU KIDS WANT TO **RUN THIS RAPID?**"

"YEAH, LET'S **GO FOR IT!**" SAY TINA AND DOOLEY.

"OKAY, FIRST WE'RE GOING TO **CUT CLOSE** TO THE **LEFT** BANK...."

...AND RUN **THRU THE TONGUE** AT THE **FIRST** BEND. THEN WE'LL HEAD FOR **MIDCURRENT**, STEER **LEFT** TO MISS THE DEAD TREE — THE **STRAINER** — THEN **HARD** LEFT TO **CATCH THE CURRENT** AGAIN, AND SHOOT **THRU THE TONGUE** BETWEEN THE BOULDERS AT THE **SECOND** BEND.

"TAKE YOUR TIME. I WANT YOU KIDS TO **REMEMBER** WHAT YOU SEE FROM HERE 'CAUSE IT WILL LOOK **DIFFERENT** AT WATER LEVEL."

THEY HIKE BACK DOWN THE HILL TO THE CANOE AND MAKE SURE EVERYTHING IS **TIED IN**— DRY BAG, FOOD BAG, AND EXTRA PADDLE— **IN CASE** THE CANOE **TURNS OVER.**

"OKAY," SAYS CHOONA, "TIGHTEN

THE **STRAPS** ON YOUR **LIFE VESTS.**

"IF YOU GET **DUNKED** IN THE RAPIDS, STAY **UPRIVER** FROM THE **CANOE.** YOUR **LIFE VEST** WILL **HOLD** YOU **UP.** IF YOU **KNOW** YOU'RE GOING IN, TAKE A **DEEP BREATH** OF AIR **BEFORE** YOU HIT THE WATER.

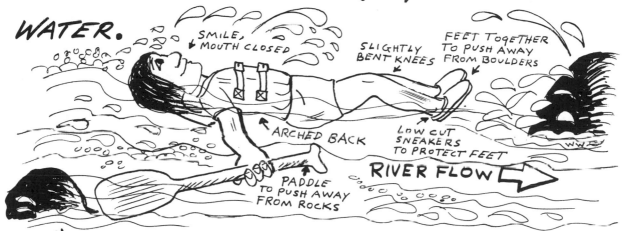

SMILE, MOUTH CLOSED

SLIGHTLY BENT KNEES

FEET TOGETHER TO PUSH AWAY FROM BOULDERS

ARCHED BACK

LOW CUT SNEAKERS TO PROTECT FEET

RIVER FLOW

PADDLE TO PUSH AWAY FROM ROCKS

"**HANG** ONTO YOUR **PADDLE, ROLL** ONTO YOUR **BACK, POINT** YOUR **FEET DOWNRIVER, BEND** YOUR **KNEES** A **LITTLE,** AND **RIDE** IT OUT. AS SOON AS YOU CAN **SEE SKY,** TAKE A **QUICK BREATH** — YOU'LL BE IN **CALM WATER** BEFORE YOU KNOW IT, AND THEN YOU CAN SWIM ASHORE.

"WE'VE GOT TO BE ON **TOP** OF IT EVERY **SECOND**," CHOONA EXPLAINS.

"I'LL GIVE YOU PADDLE COMMANDS FROM THE **BACK**, BUT YOU KIDS NEED TO **WATCH** FOR **BOULDERS** I **MIGHT NOT SEE**, AND PUSH **AWAY** FROM THEM WITH YOUR **PADDLES**."

"**GREAT!**—WE'LL GIVE IT OUR BEST, UNCLE CHOONA," SAYS DOOLEY.

"YOU BET," AGREES TINA.

"GOOD," SAYS CHOONA. "SO WE CAN **BALANCE** THE CANOE, **DOOLEY**, YOU CLIMB IN **FRONT**. **TINA**, YOU GET IN THE **MIDDLE**."

CHOONA PUSHES OFF WITH ONE LEG, HOPS IN, AND GRABS HIS **PADDLE**.

"HARD FORWARD PADDLE!" CALLS CHOONA, AS HE STEERS INTO THE MAIN CURRENT.

AS THEY APPROACH THE RAPIDS, THE RIVER PICKS UP SPEED. THEY PADDLE AROUND THE FIRST BEND.

"BOULDER ON THE LEFT," SHOUTS DOOLEY.

"DOOLEY, PRY LEFT!" YELLS CHOONA. "TINA, BACKPADDLE!" AND CHOONA LINES THE CANOE UP. "HARD FORWARD PADDLE!" AND THE CURRENT CARRIES THEM THRU THE FIRST TONGUE.

"YAHHHHH!" SCREAMS DOOLEY, AS A WAVE SPRAYS HIM IN THE FACE.

"DOOLEY, DRAW LEFT, TINA, PRY RIGHT!" BARKS CHOONA, AS HE LINES THEM UP FOR A RUN PAST THE STRAINER.

"*EEEEEYAHHH!*" SHOUT TINA AND DOOLEY, AS THEY GET SOAKED.

"**HARD FORWARD PADDLE!**" CALLS CHOONA, AND THEY CUT CLOSE TO A BIG BOULDER. "**PADDLES UP!**" CHOONA STEERS THEM THRU THE TONGUE BETWEEN THE BIG BOULDERS AT THE **SECOND BEND**.

AND THE FLOW OF THE CURRENT CARRIES THEM OUT OF THE RAPIDS AND DOWN THE RIVER, WHICH AGAIN BECOMES SMOOTH AND CALM.

"**YEA!** WE **MADE** IT!" CROW TINA AND DOOLEY.

"YOU KIDS DID **GREAT**," SMILES CHOONA. "IT WAS A **GOOD RUN**."

THEY FLOAT QUIETLY DOWNSTREAM, WITH ONLY THE **SOUND** OF THEIR **PADDLES** IN THE WATER.

CHOONA SEES HOW THE **STRENGTH** OF THE **RIVER** HAS **FLOWED INTO** HIS **NIECE** AND **NEPHEW,** AND HE SMILES TO HIMSELF AS HE REMEMBERS HIS **GRANDFATHER'S WORDS.**

SUDDENLY, 2 SMALL, DARK SHADOWS **CRISSCROSS** BENEATH THE CANOE.

"**LOOK!**" CRIES DOOLEY.

"**WHAT'S THAT?**" ASKS TINA.

UP AHEAD, 2 FURRY FACES POP TO THE SURFACE...

...THEN QUICKLY **PLOP BACK UNDER.**

"*RIVER OTTERS,*" SAYS CHOONA. "LOOKS LIKE THEY'RE **HUNTING** AND **HAVING FUN** AT THE **SAME TIME.**"

THEY WATCH AS ONE OF THE OTTERS CATCHES A **FAT CARP,** AND THE PAIR SWIM OFF DOWNRIVER AND DISAPPEAR.

"*THERE THEY ARE!*" WHISPERS TINA, NODDING TOWARD THE RIVERBANK ON THE RIGHT.

THE OTTERS **SCAMPER** UP THE BANK, **DRAGGING** THE CARP, AND STOP TO HAVE THEIR **SUPPER.**

WILLY DID IT

"GOOD IDEA," CHUCKLES CHOONA.
"LET'S GO CATCH **US** SOME SUPPER, TOO.

"SEE THOSE **GNAWED-OFF TREE
STUMPS** BY THE OTTERS?"

"**BEAVERS**?" ASKS TINA.

"RIGHT," SAYS CHOONA. "MEANS
THEY'VE **BUILT** A **DAM NEARBY**."

"**GREAT!**" GRINS DOOLEY. "LET'S
GO SEE."

CHOONA STEERS **RIGHT**, AND THEY
PADDLE **PAST** THE OTTERS AND INTO
THE **MOUTH** OF A **SIDE STREAM**.

"WE'LL MAKE CAMP
ON THAT **RISE, AWAY**
FROM THE DAM, SO
WE **DON'T DISTURB**
THE BEAVERS. AND
WE'LL **BRING UP**
THE CANOE 'CAUSE...

DEEP HOLE

BEAVER LODGE

SIDE STREAM

BEAVER DAM

GNAWED TREE STUMPS

CAMP

HILL

MAIN RIVER

97

... BEAVERS **REALLY LIKE** TO CHEW ON BIRCH BARK."

WHILE TINA AND DOOLEY SET UP CAMP, CHOONA MAKES A **FISH SPEAR.** FIRST, HE FINDS **3 STRAIGHT BRANCHES** — A **LONG** ONE FOR THE HANDLE AND 2 **SHORTER** ONES FOR THE POINTS. THEN, HE **SHARPENS** THE POINTS AND NOTCHES **BARBS** IN EACH POINT.

END OF HANDLE

BARBS

CAUTION SHARP POINTS!

LONG HANDLE SMOOTH 5 FEET LONG

NOTCH ALL 3 STICKS AND TIE TOGETHER WITH AT LEAST 40 WRAPS OF STRING

"THIS WAY," CHOONA EXPLAINS, "WHEN WE SPEAR A FISH, IT CAN'T **WIGGLE OFF.** OKAY, YOU KIDS, GRAB ONE OF THE **HAMMOCKS** OUT OF THE DRY BAG, AND LET'S GO FISHING."

CHOONA, TINA, AND DOOLEY HIKE UP **ALONG** THE SIDE STREAM UNTIL THEY ARE **WELL ABOVE** THE BEAVER DAM.

CHOONA TIES **5 STONES** TO **ONE SIDE** OF THE HAMMOCK, "TO **WEIGH IT DOWN**," HE EXPLAINS. "I'LL GO A WAYS UPSTREAM — YOU KIDS WADE IN HERE. USING THE HAMMOCK **AS A NET,** STRETCH IT **BETWEEN** YOU **ACROSS** THE STREAM AND WORK YOUR WAY **TOWARD** ME. THE FISH WILL SWIM **AHEAD** OF THE NET, AND I'LL **SPEAR** US SOME **SUPPER**."

WEIGH-DOWN STONES →

CHOONA WAITS LIKE A **CAT** UNTIL A **GREAT BIG CARP** SWIMS BY HIM. HE KNOWS THE WATER CAN **FOOL** YOU...

... SO HE AIMS **BELOW** THE FISH. HE PLUNGES HIS SPEAR INTO THE STREAM AND **SPLOOSH!** BRINGS UP A GIANT CARP.

"**COOL!**" SHOUT TINA AND DOOLEY. IN NO TIME AT ALL, CHOONA SERVES THEM FILLETS OF **SPICY CARP** WITH **WILD MUSTARD** AND CHOPPED **MULLEIN STALK** — AND A **CLOVER** AND **CHICKWEED** SALAD ON THE SIDE.

"SOMETIMES," SAYS CHOONA BETWEEN MOUTHFULS, "THE FISH **DON'T COME** TO **YOU**, SO **YOU** HAVE TO GO TO **THEM**. I WANTED TO SHOW YOU THE **OLD WAY** TO CATCH FISH — WITH A **FISH SPEAR** — IN CASE YOU **EVER** NEED IT.

"I LIKED HOW WE **WORKED TOGETHER** TO CATCH THE FISH," SAYS TINA.

"JUST LIKE THE **OTTERS**," SAYS DOOLEY. "WE **HAD FUN** AND WE STILL GOT OURSELVES A **SWELL SUPPER**."

"WELL," SMILES CHOONA, "WE **OTTER** GET THINGS READY—WE'VE GOT TO GET AN **EARLY START**."

WHEN THE MOON COMES **UP**, THEY ALL LIE **DOWN** FOR A GOOD NIGHT'S SLEEP.

DAWN BREAKS WITH A **CRRRASH!** AS A BEAVER DOWNS ANOTHER TREE.

"**WHAWUZZAT**?" MUMBLE TINA AND DOOLEY, SITTING UP WITH A START.

"LET'S GO **LOOK**," WHISPERS CHOONA, HANDING THEM EACH A STEAMING MUG OF **BLACKBERRY TEA**.

THEY **WALK SOFTLY** DOWN THE HILL THRU THE PINES TO **JUST BELOW** THE BEAVERS' DAM.

"**WOW**," WHISPERS DOOLEY, "I DON'T BELIEVE IT. THAT TREE JUST MADE A **LEFT TURN** INTO THE SIDESTREAM."

"LOOK **CLOSER**," SAYS CHOONA, "AND YOU CAN SEE THE BEAVER PULLING THE TREE TO HIS **LODGE**.

"BEAVERS ARE **MASTER BUILDERS.**

THEY KNOW HOW TO MAKE THEIR DAMS SO STRONG THEY CAN HOLD BACK THE WATER **ALL YEAR ROUND.** AND THEY ONLY CUT DOWN WHAT THEY CAN **USE**— TO BUILD OR FOR FOOD.

AFTER BREAKFAST, CHOONA, TINA, AND DOOLEY BREAK CAMP AND START OFF DOWN RIVER ONCE AGAIN.

"WHAT A **BEAUTIFUL DAY!**" BEAMS TINA, AS THE EARLY MORNING SUNSHINE FLUTTERS THRU THE TREES. EVERY NOW AND THEN THE GLASSY STILLNESS OF THE RIVER IS BROKEN BY A FISH **LEAPING** FOR A **FLY.**

THE PADDLERS FIND THEIR **RHYTHM** —THE PACE THEY CAN KEEP UP WITHOUT GETTING TIRED —AND • • •

...AS THEIR CANOE GLIDES SMOOTHLY PAST, DUCKS **FLY UP** FROM THE CATTAILS, FROGS **GRIBBIT** AND **KERPLASH** INTO THE WATER, AND A BRIGHT ORANGE BUTTERFLY MAKES **LAZY CIRCLES** AROUND THEM.

TINA, WHO'S IN FRONT, STOPS PADDLING AND LEANS FORWARD.

"I THINK I HEAR THE **SOUND** OF **RAPIDS** AHEAD."

"I HEAR IT, TOO," SAYS DOOLEY.

"GOOD," SAYS CHOONA. "I'LL STEER IN BEFORE THAT BEND AND WE'LL **GO SCOUT.**"

OVER THE ROAR OF THE RAPIDS, CHOONA SHOUTS, "THIS ONE'S A **ROCK GARDEN**—THERE'S **NO ROOM** FOR **MISTAKES.** WHAT DO YOU KIDS WANT TO DO—**RUN** IT OR **PORTAGE** IT?"

"LET'S **RUN** IT, UNCLE CHOONA,"
SAY TINA AND DOOLEY. "**WE CAN DO IT!**"

CHOONA SHOWS THEM HOW THEY'LL
HAVE TO PADDLE TO GET THRU THE
RAPIDS **WITHOUT HITTING** ANY OF THE
BOULDERS.

"I MAY NOT BE ABLE TO CALL OUT THE
STROKES **IN TIME,** SO YOU KIDS WILL HAVE
TO **LOOK** AND DO THE **RIGHT** ONES
RIGHT AWAY ON YOUR **OWN.**"

THEY MAKE SURE EVERYTHING'S
TIED IN. THEN, WITH DOOLEY IN **FRONT**
TINA IN THE **MIDDLE,** AND CHOONA....

... IN BACK, THEY SHOVE OFF INTO THE FAST CURRENT.

"DOOLEY, PRY LEFT, TINA, DRAW RIGHT!" YELLS CHOONA, AS HE STEERS AROUND THE FIRST BOULDER. "NOW HARD FORWARD PADDLE!"

"YAH-HAH!" SHOUTS DOOLEY, AS A WAVE SPLASHES OVER HIM.

"AWESOME!" GASPS TINA, DOING A QUICK PRY RIGHT.

WHOOSH! AND THEY SHOOT THRU THE SECOND TONGUE.

CRRRUMP! A HUGE BOULDER SCRAPES THE CANOE AND KNOCKS DOOLEY'S PADDLE OUT OF HIS HANDS. TINA QUICKLY GRABS IT.

JUST THEN, THE CANOE HITS AN UNDERWATER BOULDER AND FLIPS UP ON A STANDING WAVE.

"HOLD ONTO YOUR PADDLES!"
CHOONA YELLS, AS THE CANOE **DUMPS**
THEM ALL INTO THE **SWIRLING FOAM,**
THEN **FLOPS** OVER AND **SHOOTS** AHEAD
THRU THE **LAST** TONGUE, **UPSIDEDOWN.**

THEY GET THEIR FEET POINTED
DOWNRIVER AND, ONE BY ONE, SHOOT
AFTER IT THRU THE TONGUE AND INTO
CALM **WATER.**

AS SOON AS THEY TURN THE CANOE
RIGHT SIDE UP, CHOONA SAYS, "OKAY,
LET'S **ROCK** IT **BACK** AND **FORTH** TO
GET SOME OF THE **WATER** OUT."

THEY THROW THEIR PADDLES INTO THE
CANOE AND HOLDING ON TO ITS
UPRIVER SIDE, SWIM IT ASHORE.

STANDING ON THE BEACH LIKE...

...3 DROWNED RATS, THEY START TO **LAUGH**.

"BOY, THAT WAS **SOMETHING ELSE!**" CHUCKLES DOOLEY.

"AND I WAS REALLY DOING MY **BEST**," GRINS TINA.

"THE RIVER CAN BE A **STRONG TEACHER**," LAUGHS CHOONA, AS HE EMPTIES THE LAST OF THE WATER FROM THE CANOE.

THEY QUICKLY GET A **FIRE** GOING, AND CHOONA MAKES THEM **CATTAIL SOUP** AND **CORNBREAD** TO EAT AS THEY DRY OUT.

"LET'S REST UP FIRST," SAYS CHOONA, HANDING TINA AND DOOLEY EACH A HAMMOCK FROM THE DRYBAG. "WE'VE GOT A FEW MORE HOURS OF DAYLIGHT TO GET TO OUR **CAMP** FOR **TONIGHT.**"

AT **5 HANDS** BEFORE SUNDOWN, TINA, DOOLEY, AND CHOONA ARE BACK ON THE RIVER. THEY PADDLE PAST FORESTS AND MEADOWS AND THRU TWISTING CANYONS.

"**WHOA!**" CALLS TINA. "LOOK WHAT'S UP **AHEAD!**"

"THAT'S ONE **HUMONGOUS** BOULDER!" GASPS DOOLEY.

"SEE THOSE LITTLE BIRDS CIRCLING AND DIVING?" ASKS CHOONA. "THEY'RE **SWALLOWS.** I CALL THIS PLACE **SWALLOW ROCK,**" HE EXPLAINS, STEERING THE CANOE ONTO THE BEACH NEXT TO THE GIANT ROCK.

"WE'LL CAMP HERE FOR THE NIGHT."

"YOU KNOW, UNCLE CHOONA," SAYS DOOLEY, AS THEY SIT DOWN TO THE **CATFISH** TINA CAUGHT FOR SUPPER, "THE RIVER'S REALLY **SOMETHING.** IT SHOWED US SOME SWELL SIGHTS, IT **ROARED** AT US, IT **DUMPED** US AND THEN CALMED DOWN, AND NOW IT'S **FEEDING US.**"

"YES, IT'S MUCH LIKE **LIFE**," REPLIES CHOONA. "I'M GLAD TO SEE YOU THINKING THIS WAY. WE NEED TO TURN IN EARLY. WE HAVE A LONG WAYS TO GO TOMORROW."

TINA AND DOOLEY WAKE UP AT DAWN TO THE **SHREE-SHREE** OF THE SWALLOWS AND THE SMELL OF CHOONA'S **CORN FRITTERS.**

WILLY DID IT

COOKING IN THE FRY PAN.

"HERE'S **SYRUP,** AND HOT **MINT TEA** — COME AND GET IT."

AFTER BREAKFAST, THEY BREAK CAMP AND SHOVE OFF. THE LITTLE SWALLOWS SWOOP **DOWN, AROUND,** AND **AHEAD** OF THEM TILL THE **SECOND** BEND IN THE RIVER BEFORE TURNING BACK.

WHEN THE SUN IS HIGH IN THE SKY, TINA AGAIN HEARS THE **SOUND** OF A **RAPID** — AND THEY PUT ASHORE TO SCOUT IT OUT.

"**LOOKS PRETTY GNARLY,** UNCLE

CHOONA," HOLLERS DOOLEY OVER . . .

...THE **THUNDERING** ROAR.

"I DON'T THINK IT WOULD BE WISE TO RUN THE **UPPER** PART OF THIS RAPID. BUT, SEE, DOWN PAST THAT **EDDY**, THERE'S A **LOWER** PART. WE CAN RUN THAT PART IF YOU KIDS WANT TO."

"I'D LIKE TO TAKE A **CLOSER** LOOK," SAYS TINA.

"**ME, TOO**," SAYS DOOLEY.

AFTER CHOONA SHOWS THEM WHAT THEY'D HAVE TO DO, THEY DECIDE TO **PORTAGE** THE **UPPER** PART AND **RUN** THE **LOWER**.

JUST AS THEY GET BACK TO THEIR CANOE, THEY HEAR "**HELP! HELP!**"

THERE, ON **TOP** OF A **BOULDER** IN THE **MIDDLE** OF THE RIVER, HUDDLED TOGETHER TOO **SCARED** TO MOVE

SIT 2 BOYS.

"LET'S GO **RESCUE THEM**," SHOUTS CHOONA, GRABBING 2 **THROWBAGS** FROM THE CANOE.

"WE'RE GOING TO PULL YOU GUYS IN **ONE** AT A **TIME**," CHOONA CALLS TO THEM. "WHEN I THROW YOU THIS ROPE, ONE OF YOU PUT YOUR ARM **THRU** THE **LOOP**, AND WHEN I YELL 'JUMP', YOU **JUMP!**"

WITH TINA AND DOOLEY BOTH HELPING, CHOONA PULLS FIRST **ONE**, THEN THE **OTHER** BOY **SAFELY ASHORE.**

"MEREL, I TOLD YOU WE SHOULDA **SCOUTED AHEAD**," SNAPS COSMO.

"WE'DA **MADE** IT," SAYS MEREL, IF YOU'DA PADDLED **HARDER!**"

THEY TURN TO CHOONA, TINA, AND DOOLEY AND SAY, "THANKS, GUYS, FOR PULLING US IN. OUR CANOE **WASHED** ON **DOWNRIVER** AFTER IT DUMPED US."

"THE HIGHWAY'S ONLY A **MILE** OVER THAT HILL," SAYS CHOONA. "TURN **LEFT** TILL YOU GET TO A STORE —THEY'VE GOT A **PHONE** SO YOU CAN CALL YOUR FOLKS TO **COME** AND **GET** YOU."

AS THEY WALK AWAY FROM THE BOYS, TINA SAYS, "THAT WAS GREAT, UNCLE CHOONA. GUESS IT ALWAYS PAYS TO **STOP** AND **LOOK** WHERE YOU'RE GOING, DOESN'T IT?"

"MAYBE SO," REPLIES CHOONA, AS THEY SHOVE OFF TO RUN THE **LOWER** RAPID. THIS TIME, THEY MOVE **AS ONE**. THEY **PRY** AND **DRAW** JUST WHEN THEY **NEED** TO, AND THEIR CANOE **DANCES**

OVER THE WAVES AND AROUND EACH
BOULDER. WITH **WHOOPS** AND **HOLLERS**
AND A FINAL **EEYAHH!** THEY SHOOT THRU
THE LAST TONGUE INTO CALM WATER.

"ALL RIGHHHT!" THEY ALL SHOUT.

"YOU KIDS DID **GREAT!** SOON YOU'LL BE
TEACHING OTHERS. SEE THOSE CLOUDS
BEHIND US? IF WE **REALLY PADDLE,** WE CAN
REACH RIVER RATS' ROOST BEFORE THE STORM!"

A BEAUTIFUL **RAINBOW** FORMS IN THE SKY,
AS THEY PUT ASHORE. "WE SURE HAVE LOTS TO
TELL YOU, DAD." YONA LOOKS AT HIS KIDS
AND AT HIS BROTHER CHOONA AND SMILES.

COMMON SENSE

LONG AGO MY FATHER'S PEOPLE, THE CHEROKEES, CANOED THE RIVERS OF TENNESSEE. THE OCOEE RIVER MEANS "THE PLACE OF THE RIVER PEOPLE," AND IT RUNS THRU THE CHEROKEE NATIONAL FOREST IN TENNESSEE.

LONG BEFORE COLUMBUS OR AUTOMOBILES, THE RIVER WAS THE HIGHWAY —FROM CAMP TO CAMP, VILLAGE TO VILLAGE, AND FROM TRIBE TO TRIBE. MY FATHER'S PEOPLE CALLED THE **SPIRIT** OF THE **RIVER** **YUN WEE GOONAHEETAH**—THE **LONG PERSON**. HE CARRIED THE PEOPLE, SPOKE TO THEM, AND GAVE THEM WISDOM,

BEAUTY, AND PEACE. WITH THE SOUND OF HIS WATERFALLS AND SHALLOWS, HE TELLS US TO STOP AND SCOUT AHEAD. WITH HIS RAPIDS AND WAVES, HE GUIDES US PAST THE BOULDERS AND SNAGS TO SMOOTH WATER.

WHEN YOU MEET YOUR FIRST **BIG BOULDER**, YOUR FIRST **BIG PROBLEM**, IN THE RAPIDS OF LIFE — IF YOU JUST **LOOK** AT IT AND **NOTHING** ELSE, THIS IS HOW IT CAN **GROW...**

...IT GETS **BIGGER**...

...AND **BIGGER**

...AND **BIGGER**

...UNTIL THE PROBLEM IS **ALL** THERE IS, AND YOU CAN SEE...

...**NO WAY OUT** AND **NO WAY AROUND** IT. BUT IF YOU BACKPADDLE AND **TRUST** YOUR **GUT**

FEELING TO STEER **RIGHT** OR **LEFT,** YOU'LL MAKE IT **PAST** YOUR **PROBLEM BOULDER** INTO **CALM** WATER.

YOU MIGHT FEEL SAD 'CAUSE SOME OF YOUR FRIENDS OR FAMILY MAY BE **STUCK** ON **THEIR** PROBLEM BOULDERS, WITH THEIR CANOES **WRAPPED AROUND** THEM. BUT THE RIVER **WON'T LET** YOU LOOK **DOWN.** ITS SMOOTH SURFACE IS **LIKE A MIRROR** — IT REFLECTS YOUR FACE, THE TREES, THE MOUNTAINS, THE SKY — YOU **MADE IT!** AND **NEVER LOOK BACK.** WHY? 'CAUSE THERE'S ALWAYS **ANOTHER** BOULDER AHEAD.

LISTEN TO YOUR **INNER FEELINGS** — IF THERE'S A **TIGHTNESS** IN YOUR GUT , **BACKPADDLE—BACK OFF** — OR IF THERE'S A **TINGLE** BETWEEN . . .

...YOUR **SHOULDER BLADES**, **HARD FORWARD PADDLE – GO FOR IT!**

REMEMBER, WHEN YOU MEET A **PROBLEM BOULDER**, YOU ALWAYS HAVE A CHOICE — YOU CAN STEER **LEFT** OR **RIGHT**, OR YOU CAN **PUT ASHORE** AND **PORTAGE AROUND** IT.

THE **REASON** YOU'RE **BORN** IS SO YOU CAN **GROW OLD** AND GET **PAST** THE **PROBLEM BOULDERS.** THEN YOU CAN HIKE **BACK** ALONG THE RIVER AND **HELP** SOMEONE WHO'S **JUST STARTING** OUT.

MAKE A GOOD CAMP. SHARE A LITTLE FOOD, YOUR CAMPFIRE, AND THE WARMTH OF YOUR SMILE. ENJOY THE **STORM** AS MUCH AS THE **SUNSHINE**, AND MAY YOU SEE **RAINBOWS** AT THE END OF EACH RIVER TRIP!

— See you on the River

Willy WHITEFEATHER '88

RIVER MAP of WHAT's IN THIS BOOK

GRANDFATHER'S ← VILLAGE PAGE 1

CANOEING WITH GRANDFATHER PAGES 2 THRU 14

FIRST WATERFALL PAGE 4

YONA →
TINA AND DOOLEY SHOW UP PAGE 16

CHOONA'S CABIN PAGE 15

PAST THE DEER PAGE 10

CHOONA'S FIRST RAPID PAGE 6

LIFE VESTS → PAGES 21-22

GRANDFATHER QUIET PADDLES PAGE 9

HOW TO PADDLE PAGE 27
— AND —
HOW TO BACK PADDLE PAGES 30-31

HOW TO PULL A CANOE IN PAGE 34

THE RIVER
WILLY DID IT

MOOSE PAGE 32

THE EAGLE AND THE FISHHAWK PAGES 39 THRU 41

HOW TO STEER PAGES 44 THRU 48

FIRST NIGHT'S CAMP PAGE 62

MAMA BEAR AND CUBS PAGES 50 THRU 56

SECOND WATERFALL PAGE 60

TINA AND DOOLEY'S FIRST RAPID PAGES 93-94

HOW TO PRY STROKE AND DRAW STROKE PAGES 85 THRU 87

A FORK IN THE RIVER PAGES 80 THRU 82

HOW TO QUIET PADDLE PAGES 75 THRU 78

PORTAGE PAGE 74

SCOUTING A RAPID PAGES 88-89

WHAT TO DO IF YOU GET DUNKED PAGE 91

DUNK RAPID PAGES 106-107

SWALLOW ROCK PAGES 109-110

CAMP

OTTERS PAGE 96

RESCUE RAPID PAGES 111 THRU 113

BEAVER DAM PAGES 97 THRU 102

FINAL RUN RAPID PAGES 114-115

FISH SPEAR PAGES 98-99

SIDE STREAM

THE END PAGE 115

RIVER RATS' ROOST

CAMP PAGE 100

THE RIVER NEVER ENDS BUT THIS BOOK DOES. Willy

WHAT DID YOU LEARN?

CHECK ONE ✓ □   ANSWERS AT THE BOTTOM

① AN EDDY IS . . . ?

A □ FAST WATER NEXT TO THE CURRENT   **B** □ CALM WATER NEXT TO THE CURRENT   **C** □ A MOVIE STAR

② WHEN PADDLING A CANOE, WHAT DO YOU DO TO MAKE IT GO STRAIGHT?

A □ PADDLE ON ONE SIDE ONLY, USING AN L-STROKE   **B** □ KEEP SWITCHING SIDES ON EACH PADDLE STROKE   **C** □ GET OUT AND PULL THE FRONT AROUND

③ YOU'RE ON A CANOE TRIP BY YOURSELF — WHAT'S THE MOST IMPORTANT THING YOU CAN TAKE ALONG?

A □ A BUCKET OF WATER   **B** □ A MICROWAVE PIZZA   **C** □ AN EXTRA PADDLE

④ YOUR CANOE FLIPS OVER AND DISAPPEARS IN THE WHITEWATER RAPIDS — WHAT DO YOU DO?

A □ CALL FOR ANOTHER CANOE   **B** □ HANG ONTO YOUR PADDLE, FACE UP, AND POINT YOUR FEET DOWNRIVER   **C** □ CRY

⑤ THERE'S A NOISY BEND IN THE RIVER AHEAD — WHAT DO YOU DO?

A □ LISTEN AND PADDLE SLOW   **B** □ BACKPADDLE TILL YOU DROP   **C** □ PUT ASHORE AND SCOUT IT OUT

⑥ PORTAGE MEANS . . . ?

A □ TO CARRY A CANOE OVER LAND   **B** □ A BIRD   **C** □ A BREAKFAST CEREAL

⑦ YOU HEAR THE ROAR OF A WATERFALL UP AHEAD — WHAT DO YOU DO?

A □ PUNCH A HOLE IN THE BOTTOM OF YOUR CANOE SO IT SINKS AND YOU WON'T GO OVER THE FALLS   **B** □ PUT ASHORE AND PORTAGE AROUND IT   **C** □ CALL 911 AND SCREAM A LOT

ANSWERS ① -B ② -A ③ -C ④ -C ⑤ -B ⑥ -A ⑦ -B

IF YOU GOT 'EM ALL RIGHT, YOU'LL **MAKE IT!** CONGRATULATIONS!

122

A NOTE TO PARENTS AND GROWN-UPS

I'VE GIVEN YOU ENOUGH TO GET YOUR PADDLES WET, BUT THERE'S LOTS MORE TO LEARN.

BEFORE YOU GO CANOEING, BE SURE YOU AND YOUR KIDS KNOW HOW TO SWIM AND LEARN ALL YOU CAN ABOUT WATER SAFETY.

FIND OUT ABOUT CANOES AND EQUIPMENT (PLEASE SEE **THE LAST PAGE**). IF YOU'RE GOING ON A CANOE CAMPING TRIP, LEARN ABOUT CAMPING SAFETY, SURVIVAL SKILLS, AND WILD FOODS (IS IT WILD CARROT OR POISON HEMLOCK? IF YOU DON'T **KNOW FOR SURE**, USE THE TEST IN MY **OUTDOOR SURVIVAL HANDBOOK FOR KIDS**, PAGES 46 THRU 49).

LEARN ABOUT WHERE YOU'RE GOING AND WHEN. CANOES ARE NO MORE **DANGEROUS** THAN CARS OR PLANES IF YOU KNOW WHAT TO DO — AND A LOT MORE FUN!

A GOOD CANOE TRIP WILL TEACH YOU MORE ABOUT YOURSELF AND YOUR KIDS — AND WILL GIVE YOU MEMORIES THAT LIKE THE RIVER, WILL FLOW IN YOUR MIND A LONG, LONG TIME.

IN FRIENDSHIP
Willy Whitefeather
88

THE LAST PAGE

SO LONG WW

FOR INFORMATION ON CANOES AND SUPPLIES...

SUBSCRIBE TO **canoe & Kayak MAGAZINE**

CANOE & KAYAK MAGAZINE

P.O. BOX 3146
KIRKLAND, WA
98083·3146

EVERYTHING ABOUT CANOES, RIVERS, TRIPS, SCHOOLS, AND MFG. COMPANIES ALL OVER THE U.S. AND THE WORLD. CALL 1·800·MY·CANOE

KAYAKS, TOO

JERKWATER CANOE CO.

WRITE TO

P.O. BOX 800
TOPOCK, AZ
86436

TAKE YOUR WHOLE FAMILY ON A BEAUTIFUL AND MEMORABLE TRIP ON THE COLORADO RIVER. YOUR HOSTS, ERNIE AND ELOISE CALL 1·800·421·7803 OR (602)768·7753

LAUGHING HEART ADVENTURES

WRITE TO

LAUGHING HEART ADVENTURES
Isn't it time you had one?

P.O. BOX 669
WILLOW CREEK, CA
95573

"ISN'T IT TIME YOU HAD ONE?" ALL KINDS OF GREAT CANOE TRIPS — ALL OVER, CALIFORNIA, BELIZE, COSTA RICA, MEXICO JUNGLE RIVERS! CALL 1·800·541·1256 OR (916) 629·3516

A GREAT BOOK

WILLY WHITEFEATHER'S OUTDOOR SURVIVAL HANDBOOK FOR KIDS

FOR 6 YEARS OLD AND UP!

FOR ALL YOU KIDS SO YOU'LL MAKE IT BACK SAFE! AT BOOKSTORES, ALL OVER!

ROBERTS RINEHART PUBLISHERS
6309 Monarch Park Place
Niwot, Colorado 80503
(303)652-2685

124

More great books for kids!

Willy Whitefeather's Outdoor Survival Handbook for Kids

Written and illustrated by Willy Whitefeather

An entertaining and informative handbook that gives children (and adults) the confidence and knowledge they need to survive outdoors. Hand-lettered in the cartoon style kids love.

"This book takes a no-nonsense approach to wilderness survival . . . you really can't go wrong with this book." – Library Talk

104 pages, 8" x 10", Trade paper
Fully Illustrated   All Ages
ISBN 0-943173-47-7 $9.95

A Kid's Guide to Building Forts

by Tom Birdseye
illustrated by Bill Klein

Easy-to-follow, step-by-step instructions that emphasize safety first. Plans for sixteen different forts in all climates and environments, outside or indoors. Includes a lean-to-fort, a dome fort, a snow trench fort, a table fort, and more.

"This is a GREAT book!" – Chinaberry Book Service

64 pages, 9¼" x 10¼", Trade paper
Fully Illustrated   Ages 8-14
ISBN 0-943173-69-8 $9.95

A Kid's Guide to Collecting Baseball Cards

by Casey Childress with Linda McKenzie

A handy, hands-on baseball card collecting guide for kids. Filled with tips, checklists, and baseball lingo. Includes step-by-step instructions on where to buy, sell, and trade cards, what to look for, business ethics, and how to organize and protect a card collection.

80 pages, 8" x 10", Trade paper
Fully Illustrated   Ages 8-14
ISBN 0-943173-93-0 $9.95

To order, simply contact your favorite bookseller.

ROBERTS

RINEHART

ROBERTS RINEHART PUBLISHERS
6309 Monarch Park Place
Niwot, Colorado 80503
TEL 303.652.2685
FAX 303.652.2689